MW00909022

Don't Call Me Sidney

by Jane Sutton / pictures by Renata Gallio

Dial Books for Young Readers

an imprint of Penguin Group (USA) Inc.

BAY COUNTY LIBRARY SYSTEM
PINCONNING BRANCH
WITHDRAWN
218 KAISER STREET
PINCONNING MI 48650

It all started on Gabie's birthday. Sidney surprised his good friend with a poem:

> *"Happy birthday to Gabie,*
> *I've known you since you were a baby.*
> *I hope your day's fun*
> *In the shade or the sun.*
> *You're my best friend for sure, not maybe."*

"Thank you, Sidney!" said Gabie, pleased that the forgetful Sidney had remembered his birthday. "You have such a way with words."

Sidney grinned. He thought he had a way with words too. But he thought it might be showing off to say so.

While Sidney and his friends
ate birthday cake, Sidney thought
up a poem about himself:

"Here's to a poet named Sidney.
He is very, very blidney? . . . shnidney?
He kind of looks like a kidney? . . ."

Oh no! Sidney couldn't think of a word he liked to rhyme with his name.

"What's wrong?" asked Gabie. He could always tell when something was bothering his friend.

"Nothing rhymes with Sidney!" he said. "When it's *my* birthday, I won't be able to write a poem about myself. Unless . . . Yes, that's it! I'll change my name!"

"You're going to change your *name*?"

"Sure. Why not?" asked Sidney.

"Because you're Sidney."

"Not for long!"

At home, Sidney tried to think of a new, rhyme-able name. How about Book? That rhymed with look, took, and cook.

No, thought Sidney. Book is not a name.

Reginald! He had always liked that name. But Reginald didn't have any rhymes either.

Sally? No, that was a girl's name.

Suddenly, his new rhyme-able name came to him . . . Joe! Joe rhymed with go, low, and slow. It even rhymed with toe. From now on, Sidney would be called Joe.

The next day, Sidney (now known as Joe)
delivered announcements to all his friends:

Joe was writing a poem about his washing machine when the phone rang.

"Hello," he said.

"Joe?" said a familiar voice at the other end.

"You have the wrong number," said Joe, disappointed.

He went back to his poem:

"The washing machine is a beautiful thing.

In my basement, it is the king . . ."

The phone rang again.

"Joe?" said a different voice this time.

"There is no Joe here!" said Joe.

That night there were three more calls for Joe, but none for Sidney. This Joe seemed to have a lot of friends.

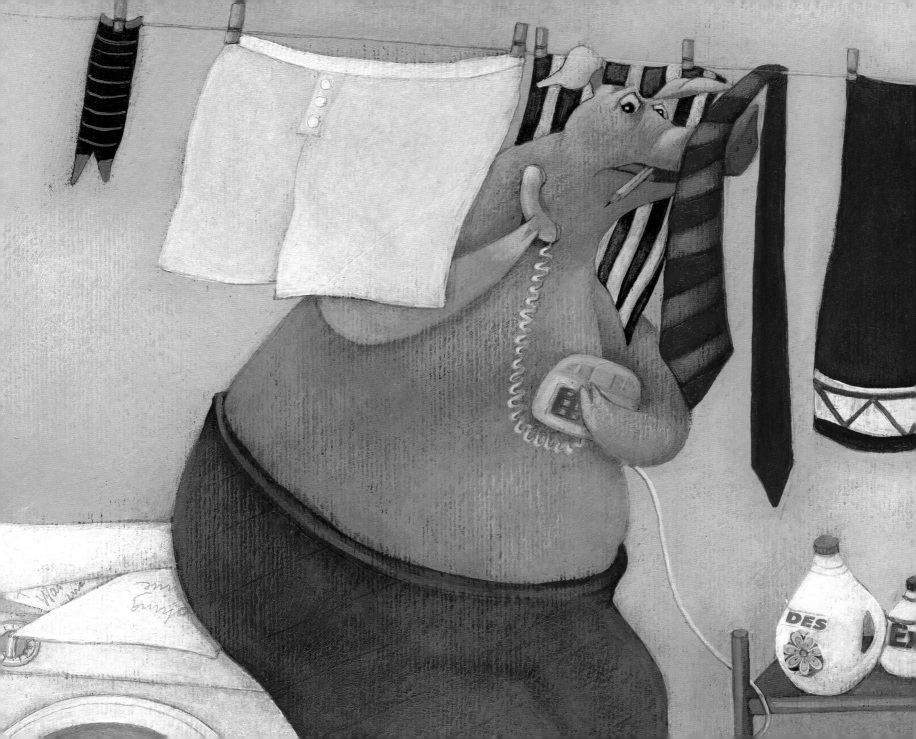

The next day Joe and Gabie went to the beach. They were building a sand castle when their friend Judy came over.

"Hi Gabie. Hi Joe," said Judy.

"Who's Joe?" said Joe. "Oh! I changed my name. All those calls last night were for me!

"I am Joe!" he said. He drew a poem in the sand to remind himself:

"*I must admit I am slow
    to remember my name is Joe.*"

When Joe answered the phone that night, he had no trouble remembering his new name. He had painted JOE on his arm in big red letters.

"Hello, Joe here," he said, pleased with himself.

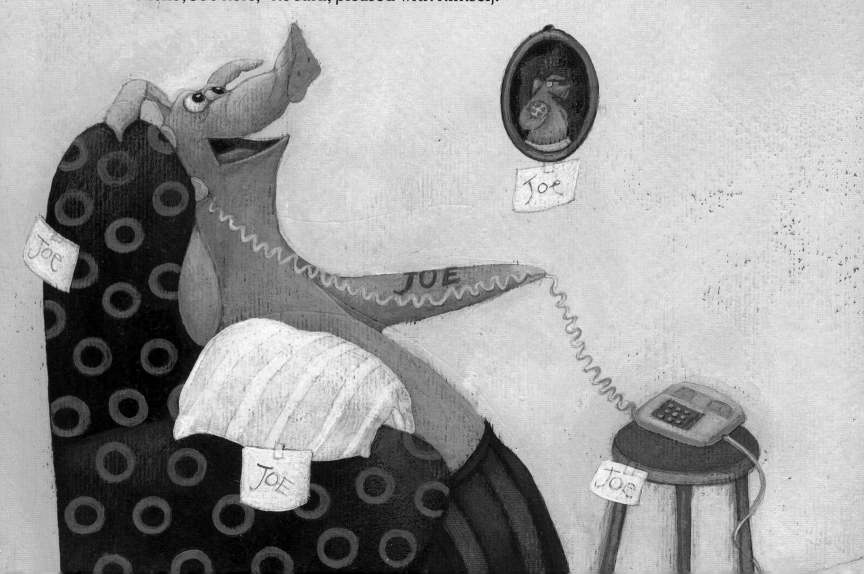

"Hi . . . Joe," Gabie said with a sigh.

"What's wrong?" asked Joe. He could always tell when something was bothering his friend.

"I don't like to call you Joe," said Gabie. "To me, you're Sidney. You've always been Sidney. You're my best friend Sidney."

"Well, now I can be your best friend Joe."

"I guess," said Gabie. "I hope I get used to it. Anyway, I called to remind you that your mother is coming tomorrow. Don't forget to pick her up at the airport."

"I won't forget," said Joe. He asked Gabie to join him and his mother for breakfast the next day. He invited his friend Judy too.

Joe cleaned his house to get ready for his mother's visit. He scrubbed the spilled soup off the kitchen floor. He washed the enormous tower of dirty dishes in the sink.

At the airport, Joe told his mother, "I am a poet now. Listen!

"I'm happy to see you.
I hope you're glad too!
Let's tell all our news.
Do you have new shoes?"

Joe's mother smiled and hugged him.

Joe carried his mother's suitcases into his house.

"Your home is very clean," Joe's mother said.

For supper, Joe cooked green beans mixed with watermelon.

"I would not have thought of this combination," said Joe's mother. "But it is very delicious."

Joe was happy to receive so many compliments.

Suddenly Joe's mother said, "What is THAT?" She was staring at the letters J-O-E on Joe's arm. "Is that a … tattoo?" she gasped.

"No," said Joe. "It comes right off."
He rinsed the red letters away in the sink.
"But why did your arm say Joe?" asked
Joe's mother.
"To remind me of my new name."
"Your name is Sidney!"

"Please don't call me Sidney. My name is Joe now. I am a poet, and my name needs rhymes."

Joe's mother looked sad. "Sidney is a beautiful name," she said. "I wish you wouldn't change it. You were named after your great-great-great-grandfather, who invented the mop."

"Really? What was his name?" asked Joe.
"Oh—I guess it was Sidney."

That night Joe couldn't sleep. He didn't want to change his name back. Sidney was not rhyme-able.

On the other hand, he *hated* to make his mother sad. And Gabie didn't like calling him Joe either.

Now that he thought about it, he was very fond of the name Sidney.

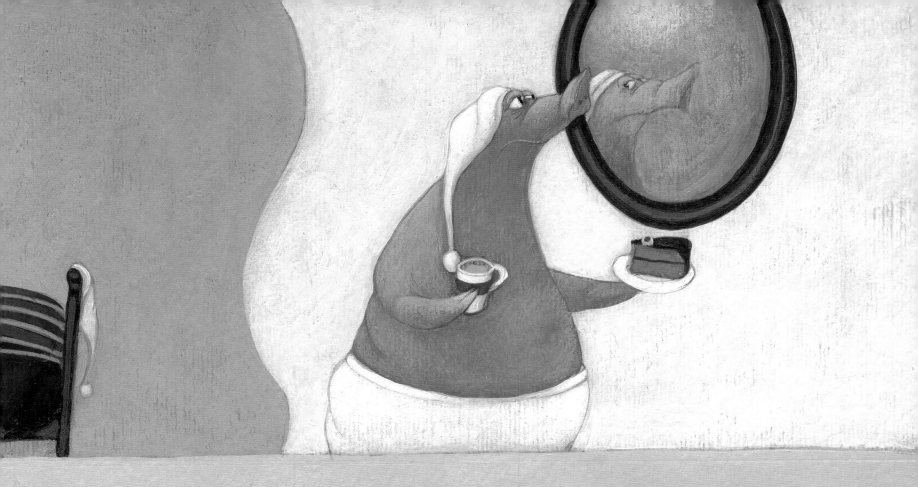

Not many people had that name (except for his great-great-great-grandfather who had invented the mop).

He'd had the name Sidney his whole life. When he looked in the mirror, the person looking back at him was Sidney. But Sidney didn't rhyme with anything!

Joe went outside to walk and think.
Names and rhymes twirled in his head
until he felt dizzy. Joe ... Crow ... Below ...
Sidney ... Didney ... Plidney ... Plid ...
Just as the sky began to brighten, he figured
out what to do.

At breakfast the pancakes smelled delicious.

"May I have the syrup . . . Joe?" asked Judy.

"Of course," he said. "But first, I have a poem to share."

He unfolded a sheet of paper, cleared his throat, and read:

"*Sidney is my real name.*

It doesn't have rhymes—what a shame!

For a while I was Joe

That just wasn't me . . . so

I tried for another new name.

All night my head twisted and slid,

Then this morning I finally did

Come up with a NEW name with rhymes I can use.

Here comes my surprising, newsiest news:

My rhyme-able nickname is . . . SID!"

"Sid!" said Gabie. "I can get used to that!"

Judy said, "I like it!"

"You have such a way with words," said Sidney's mother.

Sidney grinned. He thought so too.

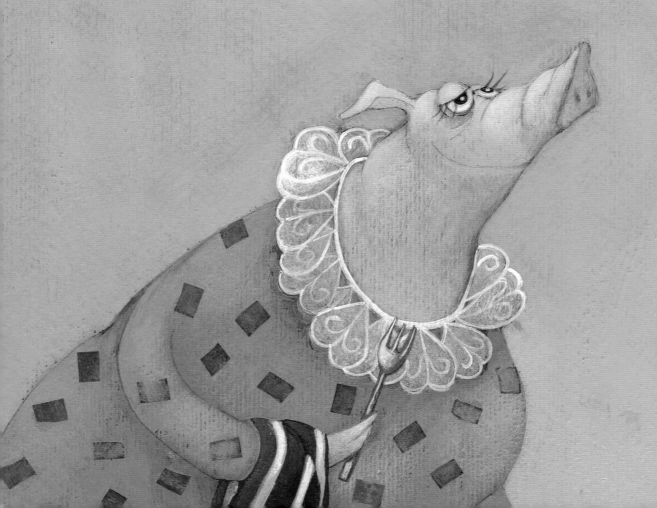

To my Charlie, who is kind, wise, and hilarious —J.S.

To my family (Roberto, Mattia, Anna, and Andrea). Thanks for all! —R.G.

DIAL BOOKS FOR YOUNG READERS
A division of Penguin Young Readers Group • Published by The Penguin Group • Penguin Group (USA) Inc.
375 Hudson Street, New York, NY 10014, U.S.A.

Penguin Group (Canada), 90 Eglinton Avenue East, Suite 700, Toronto, Ontario, Canada M4P 2Y3 (a division of Pearson Penguin Canada Inc.) • Penguin Books Ltd, 80 Strand, London WC2R 0RL, England • Penguin Ireland, 25 St. Stephen's Green, Dublin 2, Ireland (a division of Penguin Books Ltd) • Penguin Group (Australia), 250 Camberwell Road, Camberwell, Victoria 3124, Australia (a division of Pearson Australia Group Pty Ltd) • Penguin Books India Pvt Ltd, 11 Community Centre, Panchsheel Park, New Delhi - 110 017, India • Penguin Group (NZ), 67 Apollo Drive, Rosedale, North Shore 0632, New Zealand (a division of Pearson New Zealand Ltd) • Penguin Books (South Africa) (Pty) Ltd, 24 Sturdee Avenue, Rosebank, Johannesburg 2196, South Africa • Penguin Books Ltd, Registered Offices: 80 Strand, London WC2R 0RL, England

Text copyright © 2010 Jane Sutton
Illustrations copyright © 2010 Renata Gallio

All rights reserved
The publisher does not have any control over and does not assume any
responsibility for author or third-party websites or their content.

Designed by Nancy R. Leo-Kelly
Text set in Opti-Packard
Manufactured in China on acid-free paper
1 3 5 7 9 10 8 6 4 2

Library of Congress Cataloging-in-Publication Data
Sutton, Jane.
Don't call me Sidney / by Jane Sutton ; illustrated by Renata Gallio.
p.   cm.
Summary: Unable to find a rhyme for his name, Sidney the pig decides to become Joe, much to the dismay of his mother and friends.
ISBN 978-0-8037-2753-3
[1. Names, Personal—Fiction. 2. Best friends—Fiction. 3. Friendship—Fiction. 4. Animals—Fiction.]
I. Gallio, Renata, ill. II. Title. III. Title: Do not call me Sidney.
PZ7.S96824Don 2010   [E]—dc22   2008054962

The art for this book was created using acrylics, collage, and pencil on pasteboard.

BAY COUNTY LIBRARY SYSTEM

3 3243 02458 4119

E
Sutton

Sutton, Jane.

Don't call me
Sidney.

DATE		

7 AUG 1 - 2010

WITHDRAWN

BAY COUNTY LIBRARY SYSTEM
PINCONNING BRANCH
218 KAISER STREET
PINCONNING MI 48650

BAKER & TAYLOR